Coco Can't Wait!

A Story About a Girl and Her Grandmother

by **Taro Gomi**

SCHOLASTIC INC.

New York   Toronto   London   Auckland   Sydney

*C*oco lives on top of the hill, in the house with the purple roof.

Grandma lives on the mountain, in the house with the orange roof.

One day Coco wanted to see
Grandma very much.

And Grandma wanted to see
Coco very much.

"Dear me! Coco is not here!"

"Oh no! Grandma is not here!"

"Oh no! Grandma is not here!"

"Dear me! Coco is not here!"

"I can't wait any longer."

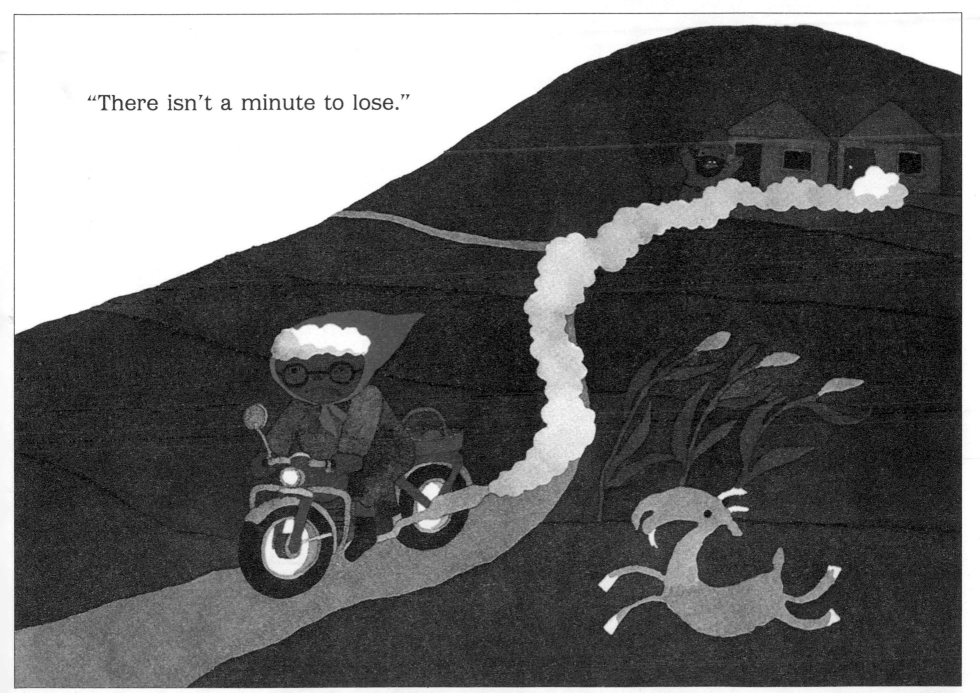

"There isn't a minute to lose."

"Oh, how I want to see Grandma."

"Oh, how I want to see Coco."

"Hello, Grandma!"

"Hello, Coco!"

"Next time, Grandma, let's meet in the middle,
right under this tree."
And Grandma and Coco
ate all the apples in Grandma's basket.

This story was first published in Japan. In the original Japanese version, the little girl is called Yo-chan, which is also the name of the author's daughter.

Taro Gomi is the author and illustrator of more than 100 picture books.
He has won the Sankei Award for Children's Books in his native Japan, and the Fiera di Bologna Graphic Prize.

Copyright © 1979 by Taro Gomi.
Originally published in Japanese as *Hayaku Aitaina*.
English translation copyright © 1983 by William Morrow and Company, Inc.
All rights reserved. Published by Scholastic Inc., 555 Broadway,
New York, NY 10012, by arrangement with the author,
care of Japan Foreign-Rights Centre.
Printed in the U.S.A.
ISBN 0-590-69548-7

1 2 3 4 5 6 7 8 9 10   08   02 01 00 99 98 97 96 95